Sally's Secret

SHIRLEY HUGHES

THE BODLEY HEAD
LONDON

Once there was a little girl
called Sally, who liked making houses.
She made them in all sorts of
places—behind curtains,

under tables,

inside boxes,

and under umbrellas.

Sometimes she took some fruit
and biscuits to eat in her house.
Then she would make a little bed inside,
and pretend to go to sleep.

Often some tidy person would
come along and spoil one of Sally's
houses by mistake, and she would have
to begin all over again.
It was very annoying.

One day Sally found a secret house
which nobody knew about. It was
in a bush at the bottom of the garden.
There was a hole in it just right for a
front door, and inside were leafy walls
and room in the middle for Sally to stand
up straight. The floor was of earth
and it smelt lovely.

Sally fetched her own little chair.
Then she brought her best rose-patterned teaset,
with all the handles still on it.

She swept the floor with a branch,
and made a little path of stones up to the front door.

Then Sally ran to ask her mother
if she could have some tea
to take into her secret house.
Mother gave her some plums and tiny biscuits
with pink and white icing, and some real milk
and lump sugar for the teaset.

Sally set out all the things in her house.
She arranged the plums and biscuits
on some big leaves and bunches of flowers in a jam jar.
When everything was ready it looked elegant.
Sally was so pleased—she didn't want
her secret house to be secret any more!
She wanted to show it to somebody.

Her friend Rose was in the next-door
garden playing in her sand-pit.
"Come and have a tea party
in my secret house," said Sally.

Rose said she would come
if she could dress up.

So Sally showed Rose
her secret house and
they had a tea party.
Rose looked very smart
in a hat and shawl,
and Sally poured out and asked,
"Do you take sugar?"

They talked about babies
just like grown-up ladies.

When all the plums and biscuits were eaten
and only the crumbs were left,
they heard a swishy noise outside the house—

Someone was coming!

It was a striped cat.

She came into the house
and sniffed all the teacups.
Then she rubbed her soft head against Sally's legs
and walked proudly out again.

A little while later a brown bird
fluttered in through their front door.
He looked at them with his head
on one side. Sally and Rose sat very still.
He hopped about, ate some crumbs,
and then off *he* went.

The last visitor was a ladybird,
hurrying across one of the leaf plates.

"That's one, two, three, *four*
visitors I've had in my secret house,"
said Sally, counting on her fingers.
"Let's stay here for ever,"
said Rose.

But they couldn't because it was bedtime.

First published by The Bodley Head 1973
Reprinted 1975, 1982, 1986, 1992
Printed in Hong Kong